Mr. Pencil, Mr. Teacher Paints with Colors

To my dear friend Hector
Ed Vieira

Written By Edward T. Vieira, Jr.
Illustrated By Lisa Delaney

Ed dedicates this book to the memory of his parents, Nicolina and Eddie.

Lisa dedicates this book to her newest grandson Parker.

Hi, I'm Mr. Pencil, Mr. Teacher and today I'm going to paint with colors. Would you like to learn about colors?

5

We are going to learn about and paint with 12 different colors. See the colors on my palette? Repeat them after me:

Yellow

Amber

Orange

Bright Red

Red

Magenta

Purple

Violet

Blue

Teal

Green

Bright Green.

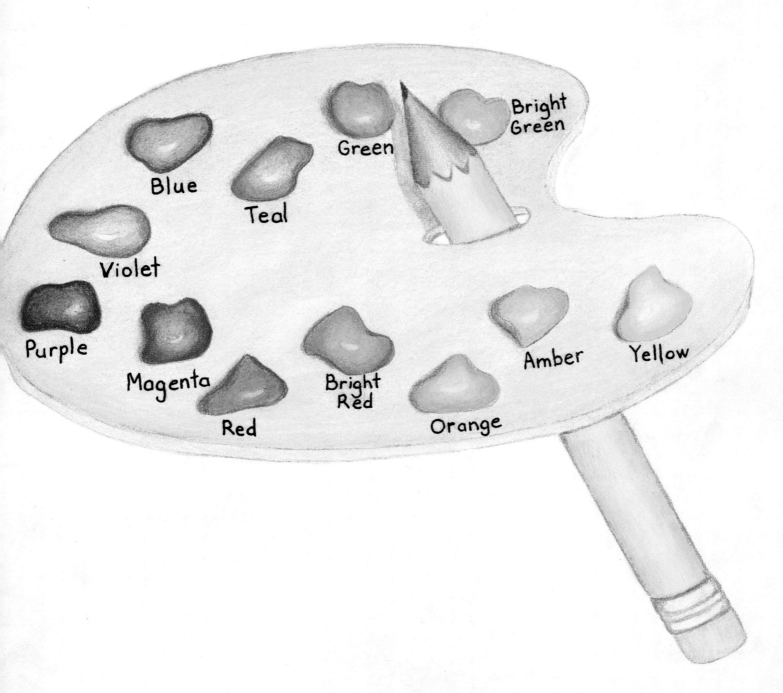

Blue

Green

Bright
Green

Teal

Violet

Purple

Magenta

Red

Bright
Red

Orange

Amber

Yellow

7

Blue is a color. Pick the blue paint brush.

8

Red is a color. Pick the red paint brush.

11

Yellow is a color. Pick the yellow paint brush.

12

13

Green is made by mixing together the colors yellow and blue. Pick the green paint brush.

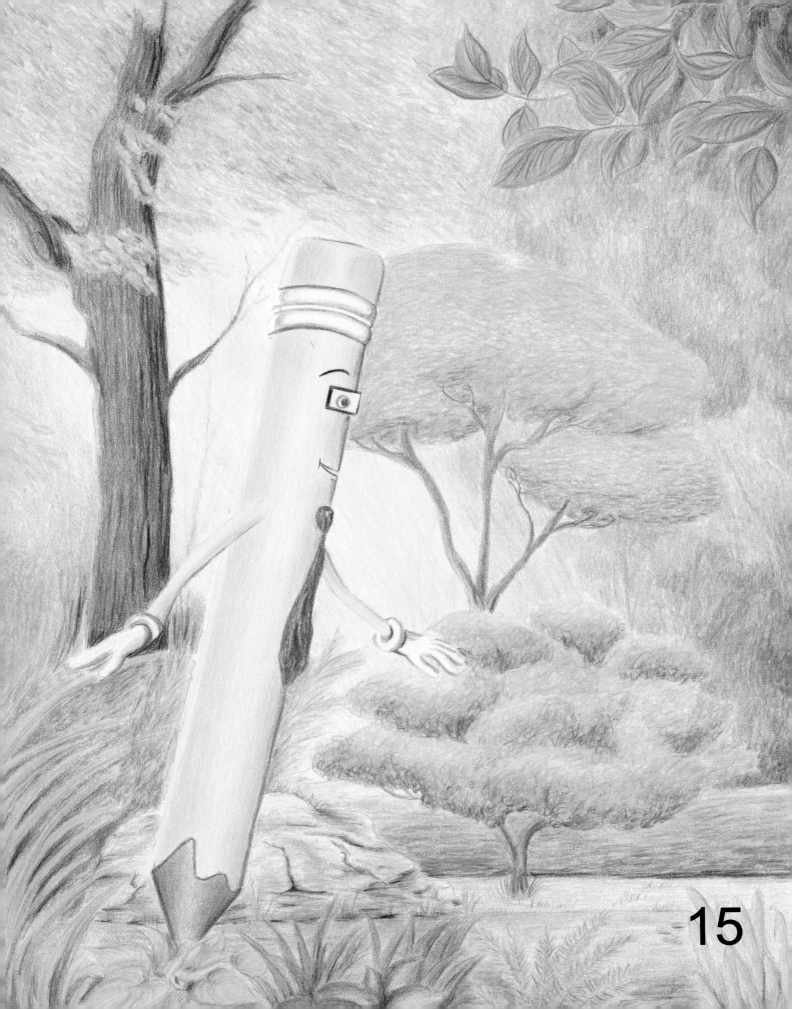

15

Orange is made by mixing together the colors yellow and red. Pick the orange paint brush.

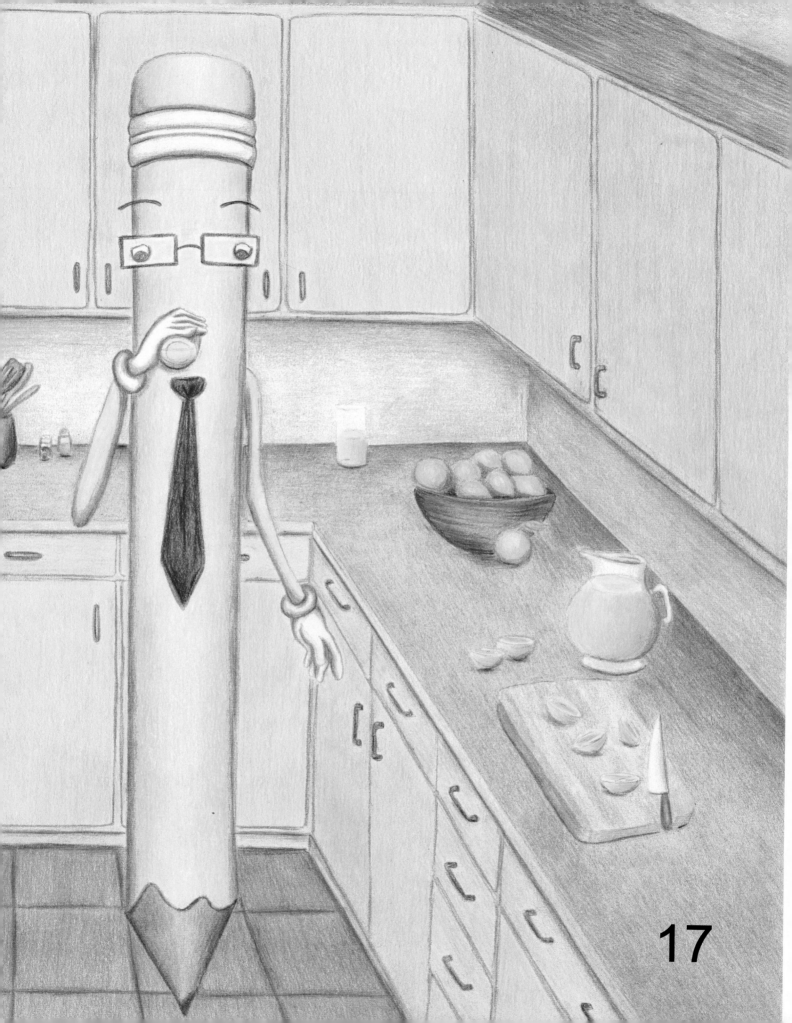

17

Purple is made by mixing together the colors red and blue. Pick the purple paint brush.

18

Amber is made by mixing together the colors yellow and orange. Pick the amber paint brush.

20

JEWELRY STORE

21

Bright Red is made by mixing together the colors red and orange. Pick the bright red paint brush.

23

Magenta is made by mixing together the colors red and purple. Pick the magenta paint brush.

25

Violet is made by mixing together the colors blue and purple. Pick the violet paint brush.

27

Teal is made by mixing together the colors blue and green. Pick the teal paint brush.

29

Bright Green is made by mixing together the colors yellow and green. Pick the bright green paint brush.

30

31

Well, I guess that this lesson got a bit messy. Can you name each color that's on me? As I say a color, find it on me:

Yellow

Amber

Orange

Bright Red

Red

Magenta

Purple

Violet

Blue

Teal

Green

Bright Green.

That was fun!

33

I hope that you enjoyed painting the colors. I sure did. Until next time, bye bye!

34

Thank you for reading "Mr. Pencil, Mr. Teacher Paints with Colors." If you like this story, please feel free to write a review.

Made in the USA
Middletown, DE
24 April 2024

53418772R00022